breeganjane

CARBIE

ILLUSTRATIONS BY VLADA SOSHKINA

Archway Publishing books may be ordered through booksellers or by contacting:

Archway Publishing
1663 Liberty Drive
Bloomington, IN 47403
www.archwaypublishing.com
1 (888) 242-5904

ISBN: 978-1-4808-8081-8 (sc)
ISBN: 978-1-4808-8082-5 (hc)
ISBN: 978-1-4808-8080-1 (e)

Print information available on the last page.

Archway Publishing rev. date: 08/14/2019

ARCHWAY
PUBLISHING

FOR MADI AND STELLA.

Your mom was one of the most beautiful,
sparkling diamonds I have ever seen.

CURIOUS CARBIE

WAS SWEET BUT SHY,
HE WAS SMALL WITH ROUGH EDGES AND
WOULDN'T HURT A FLY.

ONE DAY HE WAS SKIPPING ALONG
WHEN HE SPOTTED A HOLE
WHILE ON HIS STROLL.

CARBIE WAS LOST
AND OH SO SAD.
IN THE CRACK IT WAS COLD,
DARK AND FELT SO BAD.

FOR QUITE SOME TIME
HE SHIVERED
AND CRIED,
HOPING SOMEONE SOON
WOULD WALK BY.

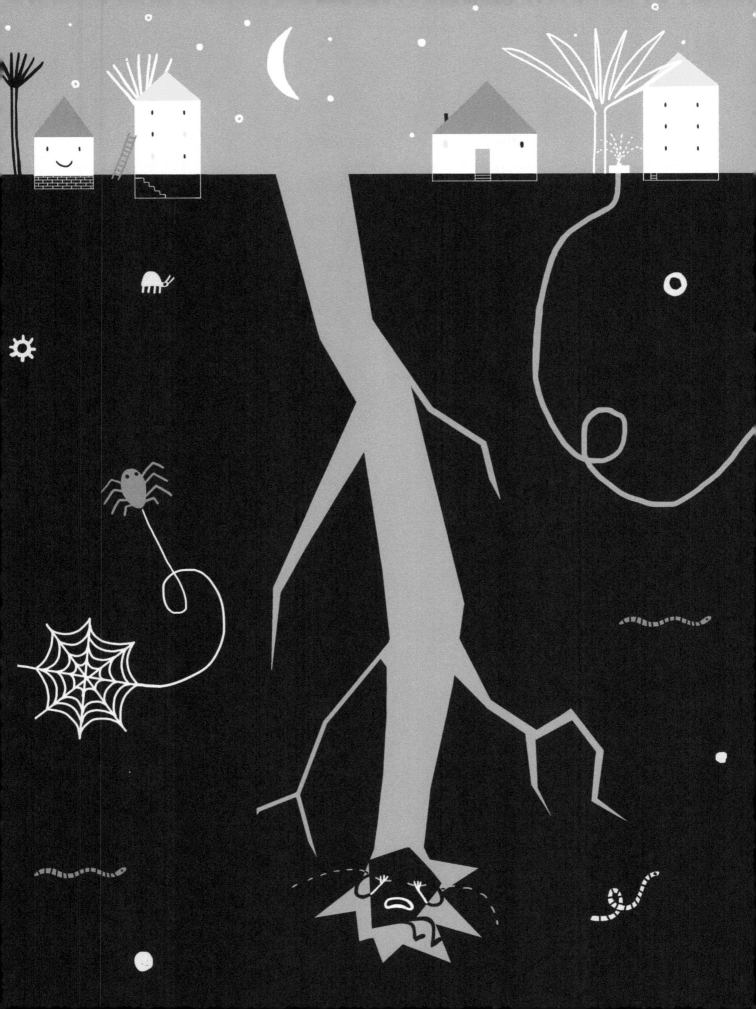

BUT DEEP IN HIS HEART HE WAS
BRAVE AND STRONG.
KNOWING SOMEDAY
SOMEONE WOULD COME
ALONG.

SO HE WIGGLED AND TWIRLED.
HE SQUISHED AND SQUEEZED;
HE PUSHED AND HE PULLED,
TRYING TO GET FREE.
HE GOT ANGRY AND FRUSTRATED.
HE FELT HURT AND SAD.

BUT IN THAT DEEP DARK HOLE
CARBIE WAS GROWING.
THE NOOKS IN THE CRACK CLOSED IN,
AND IT SEEMED LIKE HE WOULD
NEVER WIN.

BUT, JUST AS HE
WAS ABOUT TO GIVE UP,
HE SAW SOME

LIGHT

IN SIGHT.

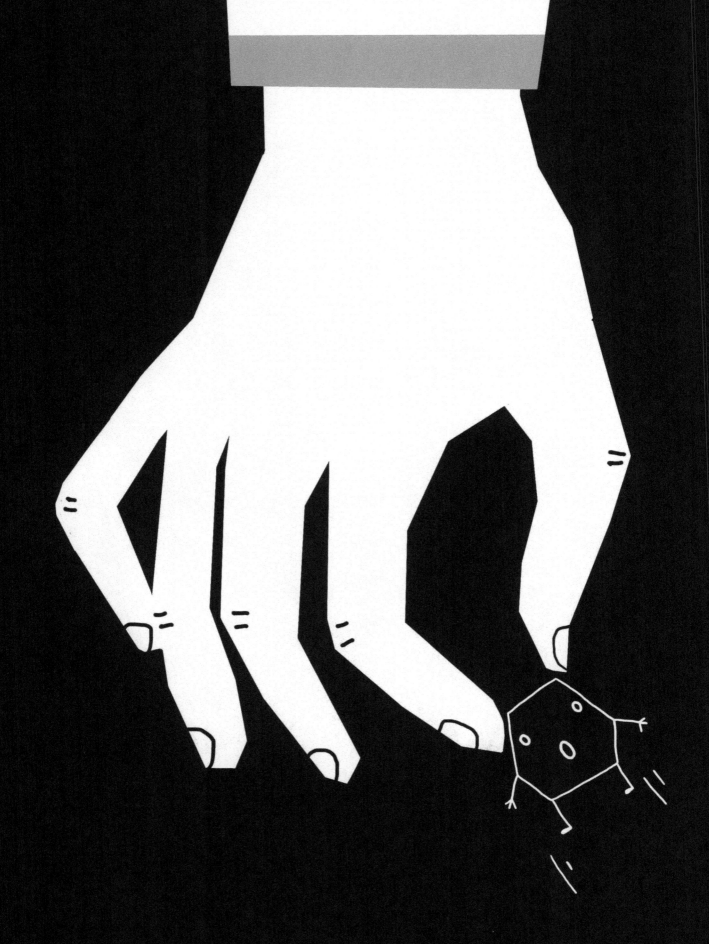

A HAND REACHED IN,
AND WIGGLED
AND TWIRLED.
THAT HAND SQUEEZED
AND SQUISHED.
PUSHED AND PULLED,
AND GOT HIM LOOSE!

BUT CARBIE, YOU SEE,
WHEN HE FINALLY GOT FREE—
HE HAD CHANGED
JUST A BIT
WHILE HAVING A FIT.

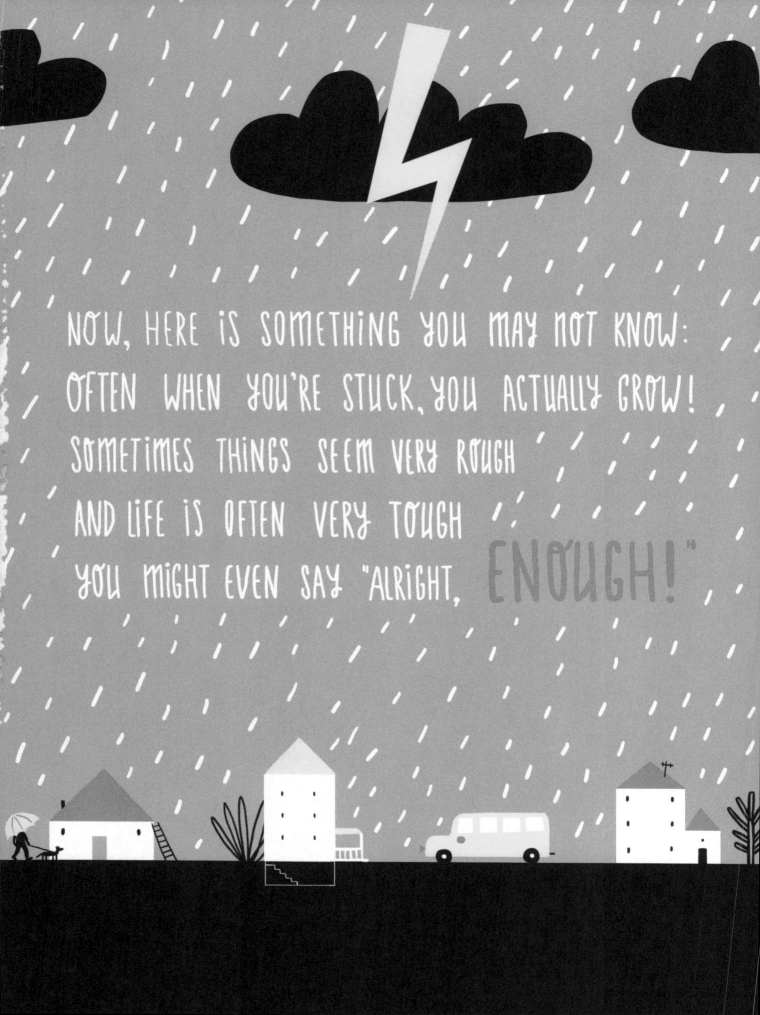

NOW, HERE IS SOMETHING YOU MAY NOT KNOW:
OFTEN WHEN YOU'RE STUCK, YOU ACTUALLY GROW!
SOMETIMES THINGS SEEM VERY ROUGH
AND LIFE IS OFTEN VERY TOUGH
YOU MIGHT EVEN SAY "ALRIGHT, ENOUGH!"

BUT JUST HOLD A LITTLE LONGER
THIS HARD TIME WILL MAKE YOU STRONGER.
REMEMBER CARBIE IN THAT CRACK?
HE WENT THROUGH TOO MUCH TO TURN BACK.

WHAT FELT LIKE SUCH A STRUGGLE
ENDED UP BEING QUITE HELPFUL.
IT MAY BE HARD TO UNDERSTAND
HOW PROBLEMS CAN LEND A HELPING HAND.
DON'T LET THE PRESSURE MAKE YOU STOP
JUST CLIMB YOUR WAY STRAIGHT TO THE TOP!
CARBIE KNEW IF HE KEPT TRYING
HE WOULD ONE DAY WIND UP SHINING!

ALL THE PRESSURE AND ACHE
WHEN HE REFUSED tO BREAK
HAD DONE SOMETHING BEAUTIFUL,
YOU'D AGREE.
CARBIE HAD BECOME WHAT HE WAS
MEANT TO BE:

A BEAUTIFUL,
SPARKLING DiAMOND

EXPLAIN DIAMOND CREATION TO YOUR CHILD WITH 5 EASY STEPS!

STEP 1

Before a diamond like Carbie is shiny and sparkly, it is made only of carbon. Carbon is an element found on our planet that we all need in order to live. It is inside of almost everything—even inside of us!

*Bonus: Examples to name and talk about:
The graphite in your pencil is carbon.
The charcoal we grill with is carbon.

STEP 2

The carbon that lives deep inside the core of the earth gets VERY hot – between 2000 and 4000 degrees!

STEP 3

While the carbon is being heated inside the earth, it is also being squeezed, just like Carbie! The pressure and hot temperatures make the carbon transform into a diamond!

STEP 4

Volcanoes erupt and their red hot lava pushes those diamonds from the earth all the way to the surface where people can go and find them.

STEP 5

The little pieces of carbon start out one way, go through a LOT of heat and pressure and come out even more beautiful in the end.

*Bonus: Ask about lessons we can learn from Carbie's journey and struggle in the hole.

California native, Breegan Jane, is a mother and entrepreneur with an innate passion for inspiring, empowering, and advocating on behalf of women across the globe. With several successful businesses in interior designer, real estate development, philanthropy, and lifestyle expertise, Breegan is the quintessential career mom who manages to balance busy work life with her highest priority and greatest love: her two young sons.

Breegan got an early start in Hollywood as a child actor and model, where for over a decade she was featured in dozens of nationally televised commercials and print campaigns for globally recognized brands such as The Limited, Old Navy, Esprit, Vogue and Talbots, among others.

Since then, Breegan's creative efforts have spawned a thriving online social media presence and a flourishing interior design business. Having honed her design skills initially as a creative director and marketing professional for a luxury yacht manufacturer, Breegan now devotes her time to design projects which run the gamut from celebrity and commercial properties to lavish restaurants and large-scale remodels.

Between frequent media appearances, Breegan has partnered with the non-profit organization, World Vision, where she dedicates time and resources to help women and children in Africa. Breegan and her family's generous support recently funded a newly commissioned girls' dormitory and secondary school in Kenya. In this capacity, Breegan travels the globe with World Vision as an ambassador of hope and a change agent for underserved communities around the world.

As a single mother, Breegan understands the importance of empowering diverse motherhood communities through interdependence, unity, and philanthropy. Throughout this and all of her endeavors, Breegan authentically shares her thoughts and experiences every week on her website, blog, and social media channels.

For further information, please visit www.breeganjane.com

CPSIA information can be obtained
at www.ICGtesting.com
Printed in the USA
LVHW07084230072O
661935LV00033B/1482

9 781480 880825